InSane

By Jane P. Eris

This is a work of fiction. Names, characters, places, and incidents are either the product of the author's imagination or are used fictitiously. Any resemblance to actual persons, living or dead, events, or locales is entirely coincidental.

Book Design by Alex McClellan
Cover edited by Matthew Peters

ISBN 978-0-578-71077-8 (Paperback)

Distributed by Amazon

4

Introduction

This collection is guaranteed to thrill you, chill you, and entertain you! So, grab your snacks, your tissues, and pre-set the cartoons you'll need to watch after this. May I suggest the ever witty Animaniacs?

Dedication

My family, thank you all for your support and love throughout my life. I cherish each and every one of you.

Mom, thank you for choosing me, for fighting for me, for lifting me up. I dedicate *I Do* to you, and your love of love.

Morgan, my twin, you are a light! I couldn't imagine a life without you in it. Thank you for your honesty and patience. Also... my child. (She'll get it.)

To my SCA family, you all are the greatest group of people I've ever met! Lady Iris sends her warmest well wishes for you and your family's health and safety, and hopes to gather again soon. Three Rivers! Calontir!

For everyone who's read everything I've ever sent them, who gave me their feedback and honest opinions, I want to thank you from the bottom of my Writers Tears whiskey bottle. It's because of your efforts that I've evolved into a better writer.

Special shout out to Bria for reading Literally Everything I sent her, for hearing all my crazy theories, and for indulging my madness. You rock, girl! Can't wait to jump horses with you again soon.

To the employees of I-hop, no there was not a body in the trunk, we were just swapping theories.

Contents

The Present

Nothing to do but stare up at my bedroom ceiling and wait. He said he'd give it to me soon, but two weeks had come and gone since my eighteenth birthday and still no "life changing" present. I just hoped for a car. I had my license the day I turned sixteen, and still no car. Didn't matter the old man was loaded. "You'll have to earn it yourself," he'd say every time I asked. Whatever. I negotiated a deal. I'd borrow one of the twelve extra cars till I could buy one of my own. I even worked on them to sweeten the deal. So I wasn't sweatin' getting a crap job to get a crap car. He promised to let me into the family business when I turned eighteen. Not that I knew what he did. Some CEO for some business that does blah, blah, I don't care. It payed millions. I'd do it. Either way, present or no present, things were looking up. I winked at my ceiling.

Dad texted. Better go down and greet him. The one time I didn't... I shuddered past the armory. He didn't like that. I tried not to think about it as I hurried down three stories worth of spiraling marble staircases. Mom had yelled at him for hours in this library. I jogged through its doors and saw the shadow of my child self, crouched outside the door, listening to them, ready to bolt down this

11

hallway to the main landing when they were done. I made it to the main staircase in record time. On my way down, the crystal chandelier threw rainbow shards of light in my eyes. I stepped aside, and the colors fell on my hands. Alternating reds, oranges, and greens shaken, not stirred, with while light from the bulb. I rotated my hand on the banister and let the colors play on the back of my hand.

The front door's alarm beeped from the outside. My feet locked on the marble. I could have been made of the same stuff I stood so still. The key pushed in and unlocked the door. I could move, if I wanted. But breaking from marble was impossible. He opened it and walked in. The light that played on my hands shined harsh on his black suit and shoes.

"Matt, I'm home!" Dad's authoritative voice booms down the hallway. "Oh, you're here. Come on down. Follow me." I met him on the landing at his command. I stood a good foot taller than him on a bad day, and he'd gotten a little fat over the years and was balding, but that didn't change a thing about him. He stomped like god on the marble floor. The chandelier crystals clinked and shivered together. He wore a rare smile into the kitchen and tugged at his suit jacket with pride. "I got your present, Mattie." He hadn't called me that in years. He paused at the table and grinned wider, nodding to himself like he was enjoying some private joke. "Well, I've had it for a week, but I had to break its spirit first."

…Oh great. He got me a horse, didn't he? I bet he did just to make me get a crappy teenage job so I'd have to save up for a P.O.S. on wheels. I swallowed the lump in my throat and hid the grimace. No matter what, I had to act like I loved it, otherwise the speeches of "How you should appreciate what you're given" would start, and he'd never forget what an ungrateful bastard I was, and would use that against me for the rest of my life.

"Come on," he patted me on the shoulder and tugged me into his side and squeezed, "I'll show you." He led me to the basement door. His pounding footsteps were no match for my pounding heartbeat.

I tried to get in when I was nine, and again about two years ago. Both times I got caught. I rubbed my back over the belt scars. Why would you keep a horse in a basement? But for all I knew, there could be stables and a tennis court down there. It could be three more stories of grand marble and smoking rooms and a Batcave to finish it off.

Dad disabled the alarm and flung the door open. I breathed deep a rank, nauseating stench of mold, dirt, and a seriously backed up toilet. I took a step back. The odor followed me. Dad waved me on from halfway down dark, gray stairs. I hadn't realized he'd gone down. He could move quiet for a fat man. I hurried to catch up, and tried not to worry about how much the steps squeaked, or how immediate the stench hit my nose. Dad hated to be kept waiting. I caught up to him at the bottom.

"What is this place?" The ceiling brushed the tips of my hair, and the laminate floor couldn't echo my voice. Surrounding us on all sides stood walls that wished they were cobblestone streets. I ducked a hanging, industrial light. Dad walked to the center of the front room, which took three steps, and spread his arms like he was blessing the place rather than presenting this as anything but the shit hole it was.

"Welcome to my workshop!" No way horses could fit in here. I could barely fit in here. I ducked to avoid another hanging light. A brick entryway behind him outlined more hanging lights and laminate floor. He walked back there like nothing weird was happening here. I followed him and tried to feel the same. Chains rattled in a dark corner to our right. Dad stalked to it. I shuffled my feet behind him and looked for any sign this was a joke.

I stopped the second I walked through the brick entryway and looked to my left. Two wooden tables, rubbed smooth from use, framed a floor drain and dangled restraints from each corner. Medical stands shined harsh in the industrial lighting; with clean and sharp tools, it stood out, waiting.

I jumped at a soft cry and swung around. Dad yanked at the chain in his hands. Drooping from weight, the chain led to a small girl from the dark corner. Her long black hair tangled into knots and stuck to her neck and face. She could have been my age. Maybe even older. Her blue t-shirt hung whole sizes too big. They would have fit, if she were fed. It was in the air around her, a quiet fear,

14

delicate and fragile, and all consuming. She didn't pull back on the chains as Dad tugged her to the table, and his words echoed through my mind. "I've had it for a week, but I had to break its spirit first."

I'd rather have a horse.

He strapped her down then aimed his attention at me. His wild smile twisted with excitement. "Come on, son." He motioned me toward him with a wave of his hand. In a daze I shuffled forward and stopped at the right side of the table. I looked down at her face. She stared past me to the ceiling. My stomach churned and I spun around to the floor drain behind me. The metal grate rusted red. My knees gave way and I swayed. "Pull yourself together," he snapped. I pulled it together enough to see him turn his back on me.

I gripped the table, brushing her hand. She looked at me. The way she just laid there under the straps, not daring to move. I lifted my hand to her face. Metal on metal screeched and Dad came back with a scalpel. He didn't look at me, he was too busy glaring at her. She shrunk back as much as she could, straining the leather straps. Repeated bruises and cuts into the skin matched up with them.

Dad was holding the scalpel out to me. I stepped back, forcing my knees to lock. He pulled his eyebrows together and shook his head. Going around the table, he stood in front of me and put his hand on my shoulder. "Mattie, I promised I'd let you into the family business. I thought you were ready. But if you're not you can go upstairs and we'll try again with a different one."

A different one… "No."

"Then get it together, son. Let me teach you like my father taught me. Let me teach you how wonderful it can be." He pulled me in by my shoulder. I cringed. "There's nothing better than that moment they realize they're about to die. You can see the determination to live, the despair when they know they're not going to, the lights go out in their eyes. There's nothing like it." The girl whimpered. I caught the shine of a tear. "You can kill her painlessly if you want to." He leaned down and grinned, letting me in on his funny, secret joke. "My first, so messy I was cleaning for days and I still found blood." He laughed. I stared at him. He nodded. "I'll teach you how to sever the connection at the spinal cord. That's the fastest and least painful way." I didn't move. "Or I could show you how to slice off the skin layer by layer? Completely up to you."

My knees gave out. I kneeled over and threw up, knocking over a rolling medical stand on my way down. Steel tools clattered around me.

"Oh, for Christ's sake!" He waited for me to finish. "Never thought a son of mine would have a weak stomach. Fine, we can start at the spinal cord." He locked his arm around mine and yanked me up. "Up you go." He steadied me on my feet before he let go. I only registered that he went away.

I didn't see where he was going. She yelped. I spun around to him holding her by her hair and staring at me. "Like this." He plunged the scalpel in and twisted. Her face flashed scared, shocked,

16

to empty, fading out faster than a blown light bulb. Her head banged hard on the table when he let go. Blood pooled under her neck and dripped, then streamed off the table to the floor. It collected for a moment, like water picked up by your hands, before emptying into a river flowing down the drain. He pulled out the scalpel to clean it. She stared at me. Empty.

"Hey!" He waved his hand over my face. "There you go, come back. You keep your shit together. Keep your mind from splitting." He slapped my cheek. "Focus! Take a deep breath." I did. Vomit swirled with the expanding pool of blood. I gagged again. "Your mother babied you. I'm going to call her this weekend and tell her you're going to spend this summer with me. Clearly, you have a lot to learn."

"No," I whispered.

"What was that?" His tone was slow, sure, excited.

I shoved him off me and staggered away. "No."

"You don't say no to me, boy! This is your life. This is our legacy. Whether you like it or not, it's in your blood. You don't escape family. You don't escape fate!"

I pushed his shoulders back so hard he stumbled a few steps. "No!"

He laughed. His head fell back and dust rained down around him as he laughed harder. "There's no escaping this, boy!" Dad walked back to the table to unstrap her. His back shoulders shook with his laughter and he wheezed in a breath to calm himself. "Don't

17

worry. The next one won't be so bad. By the end of the summer, you'll be a pro like your old man."

The blood pooled by my shoes. My reflection stared back at me. It turned to the right, where a pair of scissors pointed in Dad's direction. I nodded and picked them up.

"See one, do one, teach one. Well now you've seen. Next time it's your turn, barf boy!" His laughter cut short. I sunk the scissor blades deeper into the side of his neck. He wobbled around and shuffled his body towards me, wearing his twisted smile. Blood spilled over his teeth and soaked into his white collar. He reached up to feel the scissors sticking out of his neck. I refused to move. He lurched at me and nodded. "Good, son. Good," he choked out. He reached out for my shoulder. I stepped out of his reach. He fell forward, his arm still reaching for me. His blood mixed with her's and flooded the drain.

His words echoed, "Good, son. Good. Good, son. Good. Good, son. Good."

I turned my back on both of them and pushed out and agonizing shout. I did it again and again, till nothing was left

"Keep your mind from splitting." I gave my head a good shake, and took out my phone and dialed.

It rang three times before a woman answered. "911, what's your emergency?"

"I'd like to report two murders."

18

Neat

Three F.B.I teams tore about my house. The Living Room's lead agent walked on the subflooring, the floorboards piled up behind him, and stopped in front of me. My fuzzy, green house slippers tapped impatiently on the last untouched floorboard.

"Ma'am, we need to check under that one too." He couldn't look at me when he said it, just pointed. I turned my back on him and went to the kitchen for some coffee. While the rest of Team Living Room got to work on the last floorboard left, the other two were busy destroying my dining room and basement. Team Dining Room came back from down the hallway and moved on to my personal bar. Through the torn-up floor, cardboard shuffled and toppled over in the basement. One of them grunted with effort.

"Dang, this is a heavy one. Take that side. Okay, one, two…" My bookcase scraped across the floor.

A bottle clinked on my personal bar, and I turned to my right and watched as an agent's butt scooted my favorite bottle of whiskey off the edge. It crashed on the floor. Everyone stopped and looked at me. I glared at the big butted doofus. He flinched.

"Sorry about that, Miss Gentile." Keon came up beside me.

I put my elbow on the counter and rubbed my temple. "Caroline," I corrected.

He leaned in, "I'm here for my job this time, I can't call you that."

I dropped my arm and looked up at him. "How much longer are they going to search, Keon? They've been at it since eight in the morning; half the day's gone already."

"I think we're almost done."

The Bar Team moved to the storeroom behind it.

"The art's not here. You know that." I leaned in closer. "You've seen every inch of this place."

He stood back and shoved his hands in his pockets.

"Look, Car—Miss Gentile, we're just following up with what your Grandfather said."

"He was on his deathbed, and he was senile." I snapped. "You're going to take that seriously?"

"We have to."

A crack echoed around us as the last floorboard was pried up. Keon wouldn't look at me.

"I was too young to be a part of the heist."

"But your grandpa wasn't. He said he gifted one of the paintings to you when you graduated art school. Why would he admit to that?"

"Because he wants to punish me for choosing to appreciate art legitimately. Something he wasn't able to understand."

"He still loved you. He said that too."

"Then he definitely lied."

A crash in the basement made everyone flinch. I ignored them all looking at me and sipped at my coffee. The cat on the mug flipped them off.

The Bar Team filed out from the storeroom's antique archway. Boots clomped up the creaking basement stairs, and both teams met up with the Living Room Team in front of us.

"Nothing downstairs sir," Basement Team Leader said. I recognized his voice from the one who moved my bookshelf. I smiled at the scrape on his arm.

"Same over here," said the one that dropped my whiskey.

Keon nodded to the Living Room Team Leader, "What about you?"

"Nothing, Sir."

The only thing they uncovered was my collection of dust and dead bugs under my floor.

Keon turned to me with an apologetic face. I sipped my coffee at him. He turned back to the teams. "Alright boys, let's get out of the lady's way." They began picking up their tools. Keon took a step towards me, "I'll be back later to …help you clean up."

I grinned at him. "You'd better."

He straightened and loudly pronounced, "Have a nice day, Ma'am. Sorry to have disturbed you."

"Are you?" I looked past him to the agent who owed me a new bottle of whiskey. He looked at his feet and didn't look up as the teams herded themselves down the narrow hallway. Dainty flower wallpaper surrounded their dust covered uniforms. The daisies ridiculed their combat boots.

The front door creaked open, startling the birds. A few cars passed by at reasonable speeds. My nosey neighbor and her annoying purse puppy strolled by. It yipped at the large F.B.I. gathering. She'd ask about this later. She was asking them now.

"Just a false alarm, Ma'am. Your neighbor's fine." Nice cover, Keon, very original.

The front door closed, and I was left in silence and mess. I waited. I sipped my coffee and looked over what used to be my house. The floor was a wreck. They left a plank from the kitchen to the bar to walk on. All the bottles, that were still standing, were out of order. I refused to look at the basement door.

"You had to lead them here, didn't you Pops?"

Their cars pulled away and I set my mug down. I walked the beam like a pro gymnast to my bar and went directly through the antique doorframe. The single bulb swayed back and forth in the dark, dry storeroom. Box butts faced the ceiling, and "fragile" arrows pointed sideways on my crates. The open freezer door spewed cold clouds. I shut the door and turned to my cleaning supplies, neatly hung up on a line of hooks. The one thing they never touch. I reached for the only empty hook and pulled it down and to the right. The mechanism's turners echoed behind the wall as the secret door unlocked. I pulled it open and walked into my stash room.

It mainly functioned as a wine cellar. Backlit walls illuminated glass shelves full of wine, whiskey, rum, and assorted liquors in cool white light. The large square room surrounded a chaise, a small table, and a glass wall in the center holding for display the stolen painting by Rembrandt, *The Storm on the Sea of Galilee*. I grabbed a glass from a cabinet and another bottle of Writers Tears. My green slippers shuffled on the polished white floor to the chaise, and I poured myself a whiskey neat. I got comfortable facing the Rembrandt and took a well-deserved sip.

Reflection

"I know, but we can still celebrate like Grams is here."
Crowning my tree, the star glowed a warm yellow, shining life on the
silver tinsel, and shined down the rainbow and glitter covered
ornaments.

"Yeah, but still." My sister sighed on the phone. "I can't
believe she gave it to you. I thought I was her favorite grandchild."

I laughed. "But I want kids."

"Ugh, yeah, no thanks."

"Exactly."

She quoted Grams, "Passed through the generations, mother
to daughter ...blah, blah, whatever. Doesn't mean I don't have dogs
who won't appreciate it."

"Raven, come on. You can see it when you come over this
weekend. You could come over more often too." I walked down the
hall.

"I want to, but you know I have—"

"Work, I know. I just—AH!" I ducked away from the hall
mirror and flattened against the wall beside it.

"Ebony?! Hello?! Are you okay?"

Slowly, I leaned into the mirror's view. My reflection met me.
I stared, I spazzed. My reflection mirrored every quick movement.

"Yeah, sorry. I thought I saw a monster in the mirror. This horrible, warped, bright thing." I walked to the kitchen and got a glass of water. "It was terrifying, like *Supernatural* weird."

"Like that time you thought you saw the world's biggest spider and it turned out to be tinsel?" She laughed.

"I saw it, Rave! I swear." I gulped my water. "The monster, not the spider."

"Maybe I should check in on you." Something beeped in her background. "Ope, that's work. I have to go. Will you be alright?"

I looked down the hall. Light flashed out of the mirror. I did a double take. Gran's star reflected back to me. No monsters. "Yeah… I'll be fine."

"Okay, love you!"

"Love you too." She hung up before I got it all out.

I refilled my glass and drank half of it. Panic transitioned to a lightheaded-pressure headache. I rubbed my temples and leaned against the sink. Sunlight beamed in too bright. I blinked the after image of the window over and over, but it hovered in my sight. The headache intensified. I stopped myself from finishing the water and took it to the bathroom instead. I rummaged through the medicine cabinet and found the headache meds. I held the label close to my eyes to make sure it was the right one and took three with the rest of the water. Light-stars prickled and sparked in my vision. I braced my hands on the cool, resin coated counter. My vision refused to go back to normal. Blinking wouldn't reset it.

"You get it together, Ebony." I pointed at myself in the mirror. My Reflection didn't point back. Her eyes glowed white. She dipped her chin and pulled a slow smile at me and her arm warped out of the mirror's barrier, took hold of my shirt and pulled me in.

I screamed as I passed through. She threw me against the bathroom door behind her and jumped at me. I kicked her into the shower and scrambled down the hall to my room. A screech blasted from the bathroom as my Reflection flew out and slammed against the wall, sending several frames to their deaths. Light flashed off broken glass as she crouched in an unnatural shape and crawled fast at me. I slammed the bedroom door shut. She banged against it, but it held. Scurrying to my dresser, I shoved it to block the doorway. The mirror on it reflected my world, but I had no reflection. I was in here with her.

I put my hand against it. She slammed against the door and I jumped back. She ran into the door again. The mirror groaned as it tilted forward and snapped off its back hinges. It crashed down into unrepairable pieces. She bashed into the doorway again, shoving the dresser half a foot, scraping glass across the floor.

I ran to the window and threw it open, gripped the windowsill, and heaved myself through. I dropped my foot to the ledge but it kept going. I looked below me, thinking it might be on the other side like the mirrored version of the interior of my house. The window hovered in a vast and unending Void of darkness. I fell back into the bedroom.

The door burst open and my white-eyed Reflection crawled over the dresser. She crouched with knees raised to her shoulders and a hissed. I screamed and flailed in panic. The lamp fell off the nightstand. I threw it at her as she lunged at me. It knocked her back and crashed on the floor, throwing the room into darkness.

Her white glowing eyes, the only light source in the room, pulsed brighter with her screams. Her arms thrashed around her. The screams rippled to growls that came from the light itself as it drained from her eyes and faded away. She dropped to the floor panting.

"I knew you could do it," she said. Her voice was similar to mine, but deeper. She stood. I backed away. "Don't worry, I won't hurt you."

"You just tried to!"

"That was a Light Flash. It had its hold on me, but it can't sustain itself in a host without a light source. It can't sustain itself at all without one. I'm your Reflection by the way. Name's Yanobe."

"Okay." My eyes adjusted to the darkness. There was no light source that I could see, but it wasn't pitch black. The room had its own glow to it with muted color. "What's a Light Flash?"

"They're creatures in my world. Monsters. They hunt us." She offered her hand and helped me up. "I wanted to avoid it by staying in the Gray Rooms, but if you look into a mirror, it brings me to the other side, no matter where I am."

"The monster I saw..."

"Yes, that was a Light Flash. They can shift into any form they have possessed, but their true form is the monster you saw."

"So I'm not crazy."

She shook her head with a smile. "Nope."

"Is there a way to get me out of here? No offense, Yanobe, but I'd like to go home. This is all too ...weird."

She laughed. "Maybe for you." She toed a shard of the broken mirror. "I could have activated it for you, but not like this. We have to get you to another mirror."

"I came through the one in the bathroom. You broke the one in the hallway when that Light Flash had you, but there's one more in living room, by the front door."

"Did you have any other lights turned on, besides this lamp, on your side before you came here?"

"The bathroom light and the tree. I was checking the aesthetic."

"Okay, we'll—" A buzzing, like a tube TV had been left on with no cable, came from the hallway. We stared at the bedroom door hanging on its hinges. .

"What is that?"

"That's one of them. It's still here. We need to be careful."

"Can we fight that thing?"

"I can, with my Darkness. Once we get you home, I can finish it off. It won't get the drop on me twice."

"The bathroom's the closest mirror."

She nodded. We walked together with caution to the hallway. Picture frames and the hall mirror's glass laid in shards across the hardwood floor. I balled my hands up to a fist as we neared the bathroom. The buzzing grew louder.

"It's close," she said.

A screech stopped us in our tracks. I peeked around Yanobe. Perched on the bathroom counter, with a human body, its knees high by its shoulders was the creature she called a Light Flash. Midway down its forearms and legs the skin cracked over glowing, yellow-white limbs ending in claws curling the resin edge. Its neck cracked over a had made of light, with pitch black, large eye sockets that shared equal space with its mouth. It smiled from eye to eye, knowing it blocked the mirror. That slight lift of its head revealed a slash of a scar across its neck.

"Vain," she said. "Still pissed about that scar?"

It shrieked at her and launched itself from the bathroom. She held up her hand and Darkness, ink black, blasted from it at the creature. I ran to the bathroom. The Light Flash fell beside me, rolled to all fours scurried at me. I kicked it in the face towards Yanobe and she hit him with her Darkness again. I made it to the door and swiped my hand at the light and missed. I tried again and made contact with the switch. A screech froze me, and glowing claws yanked me around. Vain's warped face glowed inches from mine. I grinned and pulled the switch down.

I heard a crash as it let go of me. Yanobe pulled it away and Vain fell against the wall in the hallway. The light from its clawed hands and feet cracked up the rest of its body as it frantically looked for another source. Light overtook its body and converged into a formless mass of light. It blobbed then slithered away.

"Let's get out of here," I said and faced the bathroom mirror. Both of us stood side by side in its cracked face.

"Vain broke it," she said. "I'm sorry."

"We have one left." I looked where Vain has slithered off to, the living room.

She grinned and nodded. We ran into the living room and I turned off the lamps, unplugged the tree lights, and turned off the switch. The window looked over a black Void, so the drapes could say where they were. I worked as quickly as possible. Yanobe stood at my back, hands at the ready.

"There. I think that's all of them," I said.

Laughter echoed around us. The Light Flash's buzzing took over the room. The standing mirror next to the tree reflected light from Vain as it stepped in front. Its glowing claws arched at Yanobe.

"This time," it said with a hiss, "you get a scar."

"Glow up, Vain. You can't lay a lumened nail on me."

It shrieked and jumped at us. We both ducked out of the way in opposite directions. It landed in a crouch and scurried toward her. I ran to the tree and looked around for the light source I missed. Yanobe blasted Vain with her Darkness, throwing it on the coffee

31

table, cracking it in half. Vain rolled and scurried at her again. She blasted it. Vain leapt out of the way and crawled along the wall to the ceiling. It dropped on her. I threw the front table at it and Yanobe got a punch in, freeing herself. Vain hissed at me. Yanobe shot Darkness in its face.

"Find it!" she shouted.

I looked around the tree again, but everything was unplugged. The only thing that didn't have to be plugged in was…Grans' star. I looked up at its yellow shine. I had to buy those tiny watch batteries for it. And it needed a screwdriver to get it undone.

Yanobe screamed. Vain's glowing claw held her by the neck several feet off the ground.

"No!" I pushed the tree over. Vain screeched, dropped her, and caught the tree. But the star rolled off and shattered on the broken coffee table. The lightbulb inside broke, and the last light went out.

Vain screamed, its buzzing rattling the windows. Its light began to crack up its arms. I nodded at Yanobe and she opened her hands to Vain. Darkness flooded out of them in a powerful wave that engulfed the Light Flash. Steam rose from Vain and its screams mimicked a ready kettle. The Darkness inched further and further over Vain's limbs and body. Its claws had no effect. The Darkness seared the light off its claws, leaving steam in front of its pitch wide eyes. Vain's buzzing faded out with the last of its light. The Darkness faded into the shadows of the room.

Yanobe ran over and hugged me. "We did it!"

I stepped back and looked at the mess around us. Grams' glass star lay in pieces between what was left of the coffee table. The tree and all its ornaments laid in shards like the pictures in the hallway.

Yanobe passed me and headed to the front door. "It still stands." The mirror leaned by the front door, untouched.

"Will this be the same when I get home?" I asked as I joined her.

"Yes, but I have a trick for that. It's not my first tussle with a Light Flash. Sorry about the bruises you wake up with by the way."

"That's you?"

"Yeah. I'd say it's mostly from fighting those things, but I usually just run into tables and chairs in the Gray Rooms. They do not know how to place furniture."

I laughed with her. Then looked at her, fully. "Will I see you again?"

"Everyday."

"But here? Can I," I shrugged, "visit?"

"I'd like that. I'd have to ask, but if you can, I'll let you know." She hugged me. "I've always wanted to meet you."

"I never feel alone when I see you. Now I know why." I laughed, "And where all those bruises come from."

She let go and laughed, holding up one hand. "I promise to be more careful around the lounge chairs."

I took her hand and gave it a light squeeze. "Good."

She led me to the mirror and touched the corner. Darkness flowed from her fingertip, surrounding the mirror in a black haze. "Are you ready?"

I nodded and stepped through the mirror.

She was right. My house was a literal disaster. The star glinted sunlight from the living room window. I picked it up and cradled the delicate glass in my hand. There was no repairing it. Glue would only go so far. I could just hear Raven's commentary now.

I sat on the side of the couch that wasn't covered in broken things and looked at Yanobe through the mirror. She stood at its threshold and winked at me. Turning her back, she released her Darkness on her room, and mine mirrored her efforts. The tree lifted and ornaments repaired themselves mid-air. Broken glass fused together and reset itself in their frames. Lamps patched themselves back together and plugged themselves in. The coffee table's splinters found their homes as it refitted into one piece. In minutes the house looked as if nothing had happened.

The star laid broken in my hand. Yanobe picked hers up and I walked to the mirror to meet her. She closed her hands around her star, and the pieces in my hands merged and mended. She opened her hand, and our stars lit together.

The doorbell rang. I set the star on the coffee table and opened it.

"Raven?"

"Hey, Eb!" She hugged me and walked in. "I just wanted to stop by and check on you. I was worried. Wow, this looks nice."

"Thanks."

She saw the star and picked it up. The golden glow highlighted her blonde hair. "So, you're good?"

"Yeah. I'm good." I winked at Yanobe. She winked back.

Raven took the star over to the tree and, using her long-limbed tallness, secured it to the top. The tree came alive with its glow.

"Grams was right," she said. "This belongs here." She hugged my shoulders. "I'm glad you have it."

"Me too."

Token Heart

The brunette sat in the interrogation room. She hadn't moved in the twenty minutes I'd been standing on the other side of the glass. She was like that when I got here. She held the paper cup with the police logo. The coffee had turned cold hours ago. I messed with my heart shaped locket as I looked at her.

"She's been like that since last night." Det. Sander faded into the two-way mirror as he walked to my side. "Good to see you, Alice."

"You too." We both regarded her. "She looks like she's been through hell."

He sipped his coffee, from the café down the street. "From what she told my partner, she was."

"What happened?"

"Ramón said she escaped from some guy holding her prisoner. He was torturing her. She was positive he was going to kill her."

She moved, rocked back and forth, whispering to herself. I could see what her mouth was doing, but I couldn't hear. "Sounds like she was lucky."

"You got that right." Det. Ramón leaned on the doorframe. "Lieutenant in homicide said the M.O. matched a serial killer they've been tracking for two years. Only one other girl escaped, but that was in another state, about four years ago. She was a lot worse off."

"How?" Det. Sander asked. "I can't imagine anyone being worse off than that." He thumbed to the girl behind us.

"She was missing an arm when they found her. Apparently, he likes to take them apart piece by piece."

We all stared at her.

"We're gonna catch this son-of-a-bitch," Sander said.

"You'd better." I took my sketchpad and pencil case out of my purse and followed Ramón to the interrogation room. Sander stayed to watch us.

She jumped at the door opening, and it took her a minute to register it was us.

"Ms. Evangeline?" Ramón asked.

"Evie, please."

"This is the sketch artist." Ramón nodded and stepped aside so I could come in. Her eyes darted back and forth between us, but otherwise she didn't move.

"Thank you, Detective," I said. He closed the door behind him. I stayed by the door and kept my hands visible to her. "Hello, Evie, I'm Alice. I'm here to help you. Can I sit?"

She nodded. I walked slowly to the table and was careful not to make sudden or loud noises when I set my supplies down. She eyed everything quickly. "I know the last thing you want to do is think about what you went through. I'll make this as comfortable as I can."

"Thank you." Her voice was a ghost of itself.

"If at any time you need to take a break, a breather, or whatever you need, let me know. We'll take this at your pace."

"Thank you," she said, this time with substance.

I smiled at her in a pleasant, reassuring way that always put the other side of that table at ease. "Whenever you're ready."

She nodded.

"I'm going to ask you some guiding questions. Answer however you like, to the best of your memory. I'll go from there. When I have a preliminary sketch done, we'll make adjustments."

Evie took a deep breath in. "Okay. Let's do this."

I poised my pencil over my sketchbook. "How old?"

"Maybe late twenties, early thirties?"

I made notes in the top corner. "Tall, short?"

"Kind of tall. 5'7", 5'8"? I don't know. Not six feet though. He was taller than me." Her breathing got heavy.

"The coffee's not the best in the city but it's there for you, and gets the job done."

She sipped.

I let her settle back in her seat before continuing. "Skinny, overweight?"

"Muscular, but not too much, like a model. He was so strong." She gripped her cup and followed the brown swill's circle. "I can't… I can't believe I thought he was… I should have realized."

"Don't blame yourself. A lot of predators like to make themselves as attractive as possible. That's nothing to feel ashamed of. You responded naturally. That means your brain is healthy and everything is working the way it should."

"You've done this a lot, huh?"

"Yes." I pulled a pleasant smile. "And I can promise you it will help the police a great deal."

She took a deep breath in. "Okay, let's keep going."

"Was the face thin, wide, medium?" I angled my sketch out of her view, keeping the image safe in her head till she was ready to see him again.

"Medium. Angular cheekbones, like really angular, aimed right at the corners of his chin. And his jaw shoots straight back to his neck." She took another sip of coffee and checked her breathing.

"Good. That's good." I sketched.

"He had flippy hair. Lots of it. Brown or black, I couldn't tell. And he'd smile this twisted, pretty smile." Her cup caved she held it so tight. "He was so creepy when he smiled. Like smiled for real. When he took me, I thought he, I mean I thought we were dating at that point. He'd already taken me to dinner once. He even kissed me. He was so sweet. And then... The way he looked at me before, and then after, when he had me, the way he looked at me…" She started rocking back and forth.

"Evie, you're not there anymore. You're safe. Look around you. Look at where you are. I want you to tell me five things you see."

Her eyes darted around the room, "Table, door, wall, floor, coffee." Her breathing slowed to normal.

"You're safe here."

"Thank you. Again."

"We can take a break if you need one."

"I'm good. Let's just get this over with."

"Okay. I'm going to show you what I have so far. Let me know if anything needs to be adjusted." She nodded. "If it's too much, I'll understand. Do whatever you need to feel comfortable."

"I'm okay. I'm safe here," she said to herself.

I put the sketchbook on the table. Evie took an audible breath, swallowed nothing, and nodded to herself. "His nose was wider, here. Like it drops from the eyebrows. Not curved, like a straight drop, and it was shorter." I adjusted as she talked. "And the cheekbones started to angle down closer to his ears, here. And the jaw was wider in the front than that, and got narrower in the back, by the neck." The more I adjusted, the more the drawing looked familiar to me. Out of curiosity, I added a freckle on his forehead, close to the hairline on the left side. "There! That's him!" I grabbed my locket and forced myself to stay calm. He'd given it to me after a

41

few weeks of dating, when he asked me to be his girlfriend. That was about two years ago. How long did Ramón say this sicko had been active in the city? "Are you okay?"

I snapped my head up. "Yeah. Oh, yeah, I'm okay. Does this look like him?"

"Exactly."

I removed it quickly and stood to gather my things. "I'll get this to them as soon as possible. The detectives will take it from here. They're going to ask a few more questions and then talk to you about next steps." I turned the door handle but stopped. "I'm sorry this happened to you. But with your help, we can stop anyone else from experiencing this."

"That would be worth it then. And thanks again."

I nodded and left.

The processing and paperwork flew by. I couldn't concentrate. The things he would have done to her. I went to the copy machine, and when no one was looking, made two copies instead of one and trashed the sketch. I shoved the spare in my bag and added the other to my paperwork and turned it into Det. Sander.

I twisted the chain above the locket. He came home early last night. What time did she escape? I hadn't asked. *Stop being stupid. It's not him.* I made my way home in a daze.

I took my key out and put it to the door when it opened. "Surprise!"

I screamed! "Cole! Don't scare me like that."

He laughed and scratched at the freckle on his hairline. "Oops, sorry babe. Rough day?"

"Yeah."

He led me inside and closed the door. "Anything I can do to make it better?" He sidled up to me. "Maybe this?" He kissed me. It's not him. It's not him. I pulled away. "Woah, that bad, huh?"

I nodded. I couldn't look at him.

"What, did they give you trouble?"

"No, it was this girl I drew for. What she'd been through. What she could have gone through. I can't imagine anyone doing something so horrible."

"What're you talking about?"

I fiddled with my locket. "She escaped a serial killer. He tortures women, takes them apart. While they're still alive! How could someone do something like that?!"

"Babe calm down. Here, take a seat. You're shaking." He sat next to me on the couch. "Look, people do all kinds of things. You know that, you've heard it all. Why is this one shaking you up?"

"The sketch... the man... he looked like..." I couldn't.

He stood up, "Here, let me see."

"No, wait!" But he was already at my purse and took out my sketchbook.

"I don't see a new one. Oh," he put it down and dug out a piece of paper, "what's this?" He unfolded the copy I'd made and stared at it. He didn't say anything. I waited. "It looks like me."

"Only in the… face." I tried to brush it off. My weak smile couldn't carry shit.

"It even has my forehead freckle." His hand curled into a fist. I gripped my necklace in awkward silence. He watched me and relaxed his hand.

"It's not you, though," I said.

He didn't say anything.

"Right?"

He just looked at me.

"Right?" I repeated.

He looked away.

"Cole… it's not you. Just tell me it's not you! Say it!"

He looked at the drawing. "I've never lied to you. But I haven't told you everything." My breath caught in short rasps. "There's things about me that I never wanted to share with you. Things that I can't do with you." My hand covered my mouth and tears rolled down my face. This wasn't real. He wasn't saying this. He looked up at me, "But I swear to you, I'd never hurt you. Not you." He took a step towards me.

"No! Stay away!" I scrambled up from the couch.

"Alice."

"No!"

"Let me explain." He advanced. I ran. "Alice!" His stomps came up behind me and I grabbed a heavy framed painting off the wall and swung it at him. It shattered and he fell over but he recovered quickly. I picked up a large shard as he stood up. We faced off.

"Alice, this is stupid. I'd never hurt you!"

"But you hurt other women! You killed them! You tortured them!"

"I can't help it!" he shouted.

"You're sick!" I gripped the stake-like shard tight.

"It's not something I can control."

"I look like her! The victim that escaped you. Why?! Why do I look like her?!"

He sighed. "You're my type, yes. But I got to know you. I'd never hurt you Alice. I love you." He came at me and I screamed. "Stop it Alice!" He grabbed my shoulders and I squeezed my eyes shut and punched him. He grunted. Something touched my hand. Liquid. I opened my eyes. The shard punctured his chest and blood ran over my hand. His knees buckled and he wavered. "Looks like I'm not the only murderer here." Cole fell, taking me down with him. He laid his head on my shoulder, took the locket in his hand, and ran his thumb over the heart. "I'd never hurt you."

The front door burst open and Det. Sander and Ramón ran in with a team. "Police, hands up!" Cole's arm dropped and he went limp. Sander rounded the corner with his gun drawn. He saw us. "Alice!"

"I'm okay," I lied. "He's dead." Sander pulled him off me. "He said he'd never hurt me. And I killed him." I rocked back and forth. "He said he'd never hurt me." Then I remembered Evie whispering to herself, rocking back and forth in the interrogation room, mouthing something over and over from the other side of the glass. "He said he'd never hurt me."

In the Freezer

My associate shivered in the icing next to me. The bride chose her, for her "kind smile". The lining of the freezer matched the silver painted on her necklace.

"How much longer till the reception starts?" she asked.

"They delivered us hours ago. It shouldn't be long now."

"I hate waiting."

"They'll roll the cake out soon." I grinned. "And once we're in place, we'll wreak havoc on the wedding with the other demons in decorations."

She grinned back. "Like we were summoned to." She swiped up some icing and ate it. "Do you think the maid of honor will be pleased?"

"As long as we kill both of them, the job will be done. The contract fulfilled. And we can get back to warmer places." She laughed with me.

"They did say till death do we part."

Death Bunny

The creature in the photo was a well doctored, cartoon-esk monster bunny.

"I'm sorry," I told the man, "this creature isn't real. And I don't have time for your sideshow."

He spoke in a thick accent, "Please, sir, look again."

I huffed and held the picture up again. Long white ears extended out of frame, a white fluff ball formed the body resembling a fat rabbit, and its feet looked like they'd once belonged to a kangaroo and were photoshopped and colored to match. Claws curled from the oversized feet and tiny front paws. I bet if the picture were taken from the back, you'd see a fluffy tail. The wooden crate behind the man rattled.

If he insisted on wasting my time, fine. The faster I played along the faster he'd leave, and I could get back to work.

"So how did you come by this…" I waved the photograph. "What's it called again?"

"Tutzuni Ariama. Hordes of them flooded the village, eating chickens and small goats left out as sacrifice. But my village stopped their offerings. The next horde destroyed it, killing anyone unlucky enough to be in their path."

I raised an eyebrow at the crate. "So you have one?"

"Just one. Please, will you consider taking it? We need the money to rebuild."

"I'm sorry, I'm not an authenticator of animals. And we would need more than one to make an exhibit. I could pass it up the line if you'd be willing to capture more?" If it existed.

He shook his head. "I lost ten men trying to capture this one."

"This small thing? One thing?"

"The Tutzuni Ariama are creatures of death."

"Okay, I've had enough of this." I pushed past him and opened the box, expecting to pry it up by the nails, but the lid lifted without force.

"What are you doing?! Put that back! You'll kill us both!"

Long years curled up to fit inside, its claws dug into the sides of the crate, and its brown eyes widened in curiosity as it peered up at me. It was real! I reconsidered allowing it into the zoo. The kids would go nuts over this thing!

"Please! Put it back!"

"Chill out. It's kind of cute."

"Do not look into its eyes!"

"Why?" I dropped the lid and leaned in. It pulled its claws from the sides and hopped on its large feet. One front paw reached for me. I reached in. Claws sprung from the paw and locked onto my hand. Its lips pulled back over sharp, puncturing teeth as it jumped at me.

I shouted and shook it off. It fell to the floor, rolled like the fur ball it was, and just as quickly leapt at me again. Its ears splayed like parachutes and its feet aimed at my chest. Claws dug in as its front paws locked onto my collarbones. Its mouth opened from ear to ear, all its teeth sharpened to a point, and plunged into my neck.

Pain pulsed from the claws, but nothing compared to the agony of its teeth tearing into my throat. The man shouted something, but I couldn't hear. Sturdiness left my legs. I tried to push the thing off me, but its claws had curled in, holding it in place. I grabbed onto its tiny body and yanked. It only caused me more pain. I pushed hard on both sides, trying to crush it. It didn't make a difference. Blood rushed down my front. I lost control of my arms and my knees gave way. I swayed and went down.

Papers littered every surface, some still floating to the ground. The light from the window slanted horizontally in an orange glow. The hanging light swung back and forth. I tried to lift my head, but it weighed more than I could support. I struggled again and again to lift it, but my strength left me faster. I looked to the right to see the man lying on the ground, looking at me with empty eyes. My stomach twisted. It was after four, I knew that much. No one would be passing my office anymore. No one was coming. I pleaded in my head with whomever could hear me, please, by some grand miracle, please let someone find me.

A small, white puffball came into view from my left. I cringed away from the creature. I wish I had the strength, even for a second, to reach out and hit it, strangle it, something! The fur around its mouth matted with blood, and it still had that creepy smile that could give the Cheshire cat a run for its money.

Paws came up to its face and wiped fast, like a real bunny. Its nose twitched, paws over its face again, one more swipe, one more twitch. It turned its head towards me and hopped twice in my direction. My heart sputtered, trying to beat faster, get adrenaline to my body, get some strength to fight. My neck throbbed and my head swam as I struggled to stay conscious.

It hopped once more towards me, testing my reaction, landing in a puddle of blood seeping from my throat. A small sound struggled out of me. The creature stopped, stared at me for a few seconds, then turned around, showing off a fluffy white tail. It hopped out of the office and out of my sight as my heart stopped and my vision faded to black

Shaken Up

Molly Kelman, you are dead. I've come to terms with that now. I was ready for whatever happened next. I'd accepted it. I waited. Nothing came. No internal tug pulled me to some secret portal whisking me away to heaven. No light shined for me to follow. Maybe there was nothing but this. Just this. Standing on a hill, watching the world move on instead.

~

"Honey, go wash your hands and help set the table." Mom lifted the Pyrex dish over Dylan's head as he ran by, giggling like the little maniac he was. "You wash your hands too, mister! He's not listening."

Dad walked in. "Okay, what do we need?"

"Help setting the table," I answered.

"Don't do it for her."

Dad and I exchanged a grin. "How bout I help you then?" He walked up behind her and gave her a kiss.

"And I'm out."

They chuckled to each other. "Hey, Molls, go get your brother."

"I thought you wanted me to set the table."

"I'll take care of it," Dad said.

Mom shook her head, "I knew you'd do it for her."

"Dylan!" I followed his maniacal laughter upstairs. "Dylan, dinner!" He ran from his room to mine and shut the door. "Dylan! Get out of there!" He laughed and kicked the door holding onto the doorknob. "Mom, he's going to break my door!" The lamp on the hall table rattled with a metallic echo. A low rumble continued after Dylan had stopped kicking. "Mom?"

The rumble thundered and the house started to shake. Dylan opened the door and whimpered. "Molly!" He threw his arms around me. I curled one arm around him and held on to the door post with the other.

"Mom!"

The waving rolls under the ground rose and fell. The floor lifted like it was on the ocean as it rolled underneath, and wave after wave hit. Plaster fell and dusted the air. Dylan's wails were lost, the thundering from the ground took over all sound.

I couldn't feel Dylan around my waist or in my arm and looked down in a panic. He was there, clinging to me, his eyes squeezed shut. The vibrations from the ground shook out all feeling.

"It will be over soon!" Dylan made no move to say he heard me. The floor groaned as the rumbling thunder and cracking wood reached and ear-splitting level. I shut my own eyes and prayed I was right.

"Are you two okay?!" Mom cupped Dylan's face and brought it up for close inspection. She winced at his tears but hid it gracefully.

They met us at the bottom of the stairs. The banister hung on by the nails.

"Molly!" Dad pulled me into a hug. Mom picked up Dylan and leaned into Dad, who pulled us all in for a hug. We stood in each other's arms and the weight in me disappeared.

"According to the news only three people died and there was minimal damage." Mom told us over her shoulder, like we weren't watching the same news.

"Does it say who?" Dad asked.

"That new married couple, and their baby. Their whole house collapsed. We'll have to go to their funeral."

He rubbed her shoulders. "I know."

"I'm surprised they were the only ones. It felt way bigger than what they're marking it as."

Mom turned back to me. "Everything seems worse when you're in it. We should be thankful it wasn't worse."

I nodded. "I'm thankful I don't have to go to school today."

"Well, don't get used to it. You're going back soon. I got a call earlier this morning. They're hoping to reopen by the end of the week.

"I'll take what I can get." I grabbed the last piece of bacon off my plate and headed for my room.

"You're not going to clean this up?" she shouted after me. "She's not listening."

I finished the bacon on my way up the stairs and caught Dylan playing in my room. "Hey, you. Out."

He jumped and then giggled his way past me. I walked through the doorframe and the heat left my body, along with any strength. I dropped to the floor. Dylan's screams became sirens. The ceiling split in uneven splinters, cracked open to orange sky choked by smoke, pierced by alternating blue and red lights.

"The death toll has risen to over two hundred in the past hour alone. They say the earthquake lasted only a few minutes, but the aftershocks went on for hours. The highest on record for this area, measuring at seven point five. Now I'm standing at what used to be the Kelman residence. Like so many others, the structure collapsed, trapping the family inside. Firefighters are searching through the wreckage, but it's unlikely that any have survived."

A board shifted above me and groaned out of the way revealing the firefighter that pulled it free. He stared down at me in shock. "I found one!" He dug further. "There's two over here!" Firemen surrounded us. "Can you hear me?" one asked. The sirens waved back to Dylan's screaming cry.

"Can you hear me?!" Dad stood over me. Mom sat on the floor on my other side, holding back a crying Dylan, and her own tears.

"What happened?" I looked around. My room, and everything else appeared normal.

"We don't know." He brushed my hair back. "We came upstairs, and you were on the floor."

"We were so worried." Her voice caught in her throat. "You wouldn't wake up."

Dylan sniffled. "She fell."

"I think I passed out." I tried to sit up on my own. "I had the weirdest dream."

"You were only out for a few minutes."

Mom chirped up. "What happened in the dream?"

"Really?" Dad asked. She shook her head at him then gave me a nod of encouragement.

"I don't know. Something about firemen and a news lady?"

"I think the stress of last night has gotten to you. Let's get you checked out at the hospital."

"No, I'm fine."

"Molls, you're not fine."

I stood up and walked to the door. "I said I'm fi—" I took a step forward and felt my body go backwards instead. My vision faded to black. I blinked and fought the weightlessness. Alternating red and blue lights flashed through fading smoke. I hovered over firemen pulling away wreckage, huddled in a group over something. One of them set aside something small on the broken pieces of the house. It would have been white under the smudged ash. Blood seeped into the fabric, matching the costume of the Spiderman printed on the side. A shoe.

The firefighter heaved and picked something up. "He's been long gone." He cleared the way for the others to pull my body out. I laid limp, my head lagging to one side, unresponsive.

"Molly!" Dad's voice echoed from the smoke. I squeezed my eyes shut. "Molly!" I opened them to Dad shaking me. "That's it. To the hospital. Now."

Mom nodded. "Come on, Dylan. Let's get your shoes on." They walked passed us to his room, and he put on his perfectly white Spiderman shoes.

We went to the Gelberg's funeral last week and the town started to rebuild. Thankfully I didn't have anymore, "stress episodes," as my doctor called them. But I wasn't the only one. Other kids from my school had them, including some of the teachers and parents. I just hoped the weirdness would stop soon. I'd had enough.

"So what do you think you'll want to wear for the spring dance?" Tia asked.

"I don't know. I was thinking something orange."

"Orange? Girl, please remember your Legally Blonde." I hit the break and she flung forward. "Hey!" I pointed ahead of us. She looked to the empty lot that used to hold her house. "What?!" She got out of the car and joined the confused crowd. I put the car in park and followed her. We found her parents at the front.

"Oh, thank god!" Her father hugged her.

"I came home from work and the house was just gone!" Her mother shook her head as the tears fell. "We lost everything."

Their house disappeared first. The Wilson's and the Lought's house followed. People began to put their valuables in storage, but those went missing too. They'd go to add something, and the entire container would be cleared and cleaned. Then they just carried the things that mattered, and even those would disappear. The town was frantic when the meeting was called.

Old man Reed Till stood. "Well I think someone's playing a trick on us."

"A trick?!" Tia's Mom stood up. "More than half the town's houses have just up and vanished! More are going every day! My office vanished! You call that a trick?!"

He chuckled, "Only if they poof it back."

Multiple people stood up and stared yelling over their argument.

"Everybody, please!" Dad shouted. They quieted. "Take your seats. We'll hear everyone's complaints soon. Has any other strange phenomenon happened?"

A shy, mousey woman stood up in the back. "I had visions. I was floating over wreckage and I saw my body." She shook her head and awkwardly sat down.

"I had that too," a man shouted.

"Same here," a woman added.

Majority of the room agreed to seeing similar "visions". Dad searched the crowd and found me. I nodded. That mousey woman stood up again. We barely heard her over the murmurs of the room.

Dad called for silence again, and addressed her, "I'm sorry, could you say that again?"

"I think we died."

We waited. For anyone to object. The room stayed silent. She sat down.

"I don't think that's possible. We're here."

No one responded.

"What would settle this?" Dad asked.

Old Man Reed stood up, "We could check the graveyard?" A stupid idea, like most he had, but no one challenged it.

"Alright." Dad joined us and we followed the quiet crowd to the graveyard. Like ants, we followed each other to the gates and fanned out to our family's resting places. Mom led us to her grandparents. Next to it, on the spots they picked out three years ago, stood four new headstones. Dad's, Mom's, Dylan's, and mine. The cemetery had an overwhelming growth of newly dug plots and freshly set stones. Some had flowers and rocks laid on them. Each person in the town found theirs. We stood in front of them, looking at the date that marked our deaths.

~

We stand on the hill, watching the world we knew disappear and reappear rebuilt, replace itself with new. Generations of new. The world moves on. We don't.

I Do

Warning: Contains mushy love stuff. Continue at your own risk.

"We have to end it." The muggy air hung heavy on the patio, but the young palm tree and bushes around us didn't mind. "Jack?" He glanced into the room we'd spent the week in. White, tan, and blue stripped down the blankets clumped up on the bed. The bedpost decals on the wall behind it still had that three-year-old scratch from my nails. He looked away and stared down at his hands.

"Jack."

"Yeah, I heard you. I just…" He looked up but his shoulders remained drooped as he rested his elbows on his knees. "You don't have to do this. We don't have to end it. I know your situation. I know what he does to you."

I shook my head.

"Damn it, Hol, I saw the yellowed bruises. I know. You can't tell me it was an accident, or that the tanning ladies messed up. I know."

I looked away.

"I know you could be happy with me, Holly. Please."

"Don't." My cup scraped the glass table when I picked it up and took the last swig. I should have put more in to start. "Don't beg, Jack. Just don't. It won't do either of us any good." I put the empty glass back on the table. "Bill found out. I don't know how, but he did. He gave me a choice, end it or he'll kill you. And I can't lose you like that. Even if it means I'd never see you again."

He shook his head. "No! I will decide what happens with my life. And if he wants to come after me, let him. I'm not losing you either."

"Jack, please." My voice shook on the last word and I gulped down the rising lump in my throat.

"Holly."

A tear fell. I swiped it away and wished for another drink.

"Holly. Holly Baby."

"Don't." I could barely whisper. "Don't."

"Look at me. Please, baby."

I did. He beamed bright with that stupid, shining hope he always carried with him. That same look that drew me to him all those years ago.

"Hol, listen, I won't let anything happen to you. I won't leave you either. Bill can try, but he will never find us, no matter where we go."

"Go?!"

"Yes! We could leave! Together. Anywhere you want."

"Be serious, Jack."

"Just leave him, Holly! He'll never find us! I swear you will be safe. I'll take you anywhere you want to go baby. What about Acapulco? You always talk about going there."

"You're talking about a life together. I'm still married."

"To a monster."

I couldn't argue that.

"We've had years together now. I want a life with you! The whole thing. Leave with me, Holly. We could travel the world together. Find a home of our own!" He stood up from the plastic chair the staff had brought in from the pool area after we'd accidentally broken the old one. Who knew it couldn't hold two people at once? "What about Italy?"

"You're crazy."

"Egypt? We could discover tombs and become rich explorers." He pulled his arms up and flexed his wrists at sharp angles, badly imitating the Egyptian dance. A laugh bubbled up but I played it off like a cough. It didn't fool him one bit. "Marrakesh!" He sat down next to me. "Yes, we could go there. I know you've always wanted to go to Morocco." He continued before I could bring up any doubts, or anything that could bring us back to reality. "Paris? We could get married in Paris. I'll take cooking classes, be your personal cuisinier." I laughed at his horrible pronunciation. "Come on, mon cherie."

"It's mon cher, darling."

"Yes, mon cher amour, come!" He picked me up off the lounge chair and swung me around the patio. "The city of love awaits us." He pulled me into his arms, and I fell into our pattern of comfort. "We can get a, what's it called? The grand houses the rich ones had before they were all beheaded?"

I laughed. "Château."

"Yes. We'll get one of those that I can fix up real nice for you." He took my hand and swayed us back and forth. "You can live like a French queen." I rolled my eyes. He spun and dipped me. I laughed as he pulled me up and I settled into his shoulder. We continued to sway. "I can dig you a garden, build you a green house." He gave my hand a light squeeze.

"I could get a job teaching."

"I'm sure someone in Paris needs an accountant."

"My numbers man." His breath of relief blew across my face. He kissed my forehead. "I'd come home with flowers."

"Dinner would be ready."

"We could watch French Television, and I'd talk over it asking you to translate."

"And I'd eventually buy you a French dictionary."

He laughed. "We could vacation in Morocco."

"And have the neighbors over for dinner."

"No more hiding. No more having to leave each other." He stopped dancing and took my shoulders. "We could do it, you know. We could leave." He took my face so tenderly in his hands, "And you will be safe, and happy, all the days of our lives."

"How can you guarantee that?"

"Do you love me?"

I pulled him into a kiss. "Of course I love you, Jack."

"So, do you want to then? Start our lives together?"

What he offered was a dream. A wonderful dream. A hope living on a cloud, like he did. I thought of my bag on the bed, already packed, and of my passport stuffed into the side pocket. I took his hand. "I do."

Happy Birthday

My foam nose tickled, and I sneezed it off, sending it bouncing and rolling toward the yellow daisy cake. I caught up to it and stuck it back on. Not like it could get dirty, Mrs. Rhonestien kept a spotless house.

I leaned on the counter. Through the glass doors, Mike pulled a rubber chicken out of his clown hat with flourish. The kids stared. ~Crickets~ Mrs. Rhonestien and her husband traded looks. They paid for party clowns, not magicians.

From the private garden side of the house, the "Ugly Uncle" (another mom's words, not mine) walked back around, tucking his phone in his pocket. As he came up beside the party parents he cheered and clapped. Mr. Rhonestien rolled his eyes, but his wife smiled at her brother. She'd introduced me to him earlier. Creepy dude.

He sat at the back of the kid's group. Mike pulled the tail end of roped handkerchiefs from his sleeve, and pulled, and pulled. He was the only one that clapped. The kids around him shot him weird looks.

"Come on kids, cheer! He's doing good, right?'

"No!" one shouted.

"Come on." He clapped as more multicolored handkerchiefs came from his sleeve. The kids started to clap. "There we go! Yay!"

They started to clap for real. Mike flashed a quick smile to me and I gave him a thumbs up.

The hoops on my yellow, polka dotted pants wobbled. I glanced down to see Emily, the birthday girl, tugging on them. Her pink, princess dress leaked glitter as she swayed back and forth; a trail led from the backyard.

"I like your show way better than his."

I pantomimed a laugh.

"Do you talk?"

Nodding, I said, "No."

She giggled, then eyed the confectionery covered counter. "Can I have one of those cookies?"

I looked at her parents. The uncle walked back to them and they were distracted. "Are you supposed to have one now?"

She nodded. "No."

I grinned and handed her the biggest one. She gasped through a smile rivaling my clown makeup as she gripped the yellow frosted cookie.

"Thanks, Ruffles!" She ran back to the party, shedding pink glitter with every prance. My phone buzzed in my real pants. I checked out of habit.

Proximity Alert

A target was within one mile of my position. I opened it with my thumb print and read.

Target: Ray Cooper
Bounty: $300,000 DEAD

Okay, not bad. But I was busy. Someone else could take it. I kept half-reading, scrolling through the description, years active, associates – an additional 50,000 each. Then I read what he was on here for.

Designation: Child Abuser/Child Trafficker

I hit the accept button and in five strides was in the bathroom smearing cold cream all over my face and wiping off my makeup with wet wipes. I undid my suspenders and kicked off the red shoes and hooped pants. My street clothes underneath didn't need adjusting. The matching red wig topped the pile and I tossed the foam nose in that direction. I smoothed my ponytail and slipped on my pre-tied tennis shoes.

My phone buzzed on the counter. I opened the app with my thumb print and read the pickup notification. The car was waiting outside.

I ducked back up the hallway to the kitchen. The kids cheered the flags still coming out of Mike's sleeve. I swiped my finger on the bottom tier of frosting and tasted lemon as I slipped out the front door unseen.

Luxurious cars covered the driveway bumper to bumper. My ride was the only black sedan, parked one house down. I nodded to the driver's window as I got in.

Waiting on the seat next to me was a familiar black canvas duffel bag. My hand glided across the cold, black leather seat and the soft stitching to the zipper hanging from the bag. I flicked it and it tinked, metal on metal. I smiled to myself.

"Why do you never wear makeup?" So it was Harry today.

"My makeup would terrify you."

He shrugged. "Just think you should put more effort into how you look, is all."

"Ah-huh. And, how long did it take to put all that gel in your hair? Three hours?"

"Yeah, whatever."

I laughed.

He turned the corner.

"Do you know where he was last seen? It didn't say in the file."

"Party, 'bout twenty minutes ago. Should still be there. Just reload the app when you nest."

I nodded.

"Get ready. We'll be there in five."

Everything I needed for the job was inside the bag: a tarp, "cleaning solution" ammonia spray, plastic gloves, and a black case that contained my rifle. I put on the gloves and checked over the gear. I found some spare baggies for shell casings tucked into a corner of the bag. I grabbed them and let it rain over Harry's shoulder. He laughed.

"Think I'll miss?" I asked.

"That was Rick. I know you never miss." He pulled up to an abandoned building.

"Hey, do me a favor?" I asked. "Get me a yellow balloon."

The mirror outlined Harry's eyes as he spoke, "Eighth floor, northwest, one thousand meters. Ten minutes."

"Be back in eight." I winked, grabbed the bag, and got out.

The building's absence of rats, trash, and tags told me it was recently abandoned. The eighth floor was another empty, tiled lobby surrounded on all sides by an outdoor wraparound.

I walked out the northwest door and set up at the balcony's edge. The canvas tarp laid a ten by ten workspace. Assembling the gun was like folding laundry. The view of the city was stunning, and the weather! I checked my phone. Finally, they updated his location!

I laid down and propped the gun on the bag and scanned through the scope. ...wonder if Mike was still pulling handkerchiefs from his sleeve.

I found the neighborhood quickly. He paced back and forth, shouting on the phone. I made my adjustments and steadied myself. He stopped pacing. His lips formed the words, "I don't care. Do it!" I pulled the trigger.

I checked through the scope just in time to see his thumb press "end call", and a pink mist puff from his head. The side of the house was painted.

The timer in my head began as I disassembled the gun and stuck it back in the case's foam cutouts. I rolled up the tarp and shoved it all in the duffel, then sprayed the area with the cleaning solution and tossed that in the bag too. I zipped it up and scanned the area before heading back to the car.

"Smooth sailing?"

"Like clouds at sunset."

He nodded, understanding, then turned the wheel. "I think I found what you wanted." He pulled a string attached to a huge yellow balloon and handed it to me. "What's it for?"

"Someone special."

I snuck back to the bathroom to clown up. It didn't take me long. Like putting the gun together, I could put my makeup on with the ease of muscle memory.

Back in the kitchen, Mrs. Rhonestien pushed the number seven candle in the top tier of the yellow cake. My finger mark had been fixed.

"How was your break?" she asked.

"Hit the spot."

"Oh, where'd you get the balloon?" She smiled as she picked up the lighter and aimed it at the candle.

Screams echoed from the backyard. She dropped the lighter and ran outside. I followed at a walking pace, swiping another finger full of lemony buttercream.

"Okay, kids," Mike said, "let's go inside for some cake! Who wants cake?" They all shouted their excitement, and majority of the parents followed him and the kids inside.

Mrs. Rhonestien turned the corner to the side of the house's private garden, where a shocked mom stood frozen. Legs, like the Wicked Witch of the East, poked out from around the corner sheathed in black pants and leather shoes.

"Oh my gosh, Stacey, what happened? Sir, are you okay?" She stumbled to a stop when she saw who it was and regarded the red sprayed wall. "Ray?" She dropped to her knees as she shook him. He wouldn't wake. I never miss. "Ray!"

Someone tugged my polka dot pants.

"Is Uncle Ray dead?" Emily looked up expectantly.

I nodded.

"Why?" It was a matter of fact question.

75

"Because he was a bad person. Maybe not to you, but he was a villain in other kid's stories."

Mrs. Rhonestien clung to her husband in hysteria. Emily looked at them without expression. "He was a villain in my story. I never told Mommy that." She smoothed her skirt. Pink glitter rained down around her. "It's our secret, okay Ruffles?"

"Okay. Our secret."

Her mom collapsed into Mr. Rhonestien's arms, sobbing. Emily let out a sigh of relief.

"Here, this for you." I handed her the balloon.

She wiped her face dry and latched onto the yellow curling ribbon with the same smile she gave the cookie.

"Happy Birthday."

My Hero

A continuation of "Happy Birthday"

"Hold the door." I jogged to the redhead leaving the apartment tower. She kept walking, letting the door slip from her fingers. I ran to catch it.

"Thanks."

She lifted her nose at my sarcasm and clicked away into the daily crowd on the street. I slipped inside.

Along the wall of the entry hall, mailbox 1004 waited for me unlocked with the key taped to the top, just like they said. I paced my steps in the marble lobby and took an empty elevator ten floors up. A couple passed me in the hallway, and I nodded at them. They waved back as I unlocked the apartment.

Sprawled out and decked out, the dining room-kitchen combo served as the entry, with a living room to my left. It smelled too clean to be lived in. This was a display suite. I dropped my purse and walked straight ahead to the dining room table, where a tall window haloed my black canvas duffel bag in yellow sunlight.

As always, the bag had everything I needed inside. I snapped on the plastic gloves and unlocked the phone. The app actually worked the first time. Shocker. I grinned at the photo of my target and scrolled through her file. She would be at work, just over twelve hundred meters out. I pulled out the black case that held my rifle and assembled it.

Fighting for this job was so worth it. Anyone connected to Ray's business was mine. I pulled open the window and got situated on the table. His accountant, the one that processed his "sales", came into view, messing with her black suit jacket. I made my adjustments. She walked back and forth in her office with too many potted plants. Finally, she stood still behind her desk. Gotcha. A man walked into her office and I relaxed my finger. They started to argue. Come on dude, leave. I'll take care of it.

"Hey, Ruffles!" My spine froze at the familiar child's voice and the faint scent of hairspray.

I turned around. "Emily?!"

She pranced to me on her tiptoes. Her pink ballet slippers tapped the tile and her pink tutu bounced with every step. "Whatcha doin?"

I got off the table and positioned myself in front so she wouldn't see the gun. "Well, I'm... What are you doing?"

She hugged me. "I followed you from my dance studio." She looked around me and I moved in her way. "Where's your clown stuff?"

"I'm not a clown today, I'm at my... other job."

She pouted.

"How did you know it was me?"

She pushed up on her tiptoes. "I saw you leave my party looking like you, not Ruffles the clown. I remember. So I followed you."

"You shouldn't have done that. It's not safe." She dipped her chin. "I'm impressed. You should head back though," I glanced at my gun, "but I can't take you."

She put her hands on her popped hip and tilted her head. "I'm not a little kid anymore. I'm seven now, I can be by myself. I'm staying with you."

"No, you can't."

"I said," she raised her voice, "I'm staying with you!"

I crossed my arms, "Emily—"

She mimicked me, "Ruffles."

I dropped my arms and leaned on the table. "It's really not safe, you need to go back.

"You're here, so I'm safe."

I sighed. "You're not going anywhere, are you?"

She shook her head smiling.

My timeline was closing. "I guess you can stay. But this has to be our secret."

"Okay!"

"And you have to wear these." I reached in the bag and pulled out the extra pair of noise cancelling headphones. I put them on her and adjusted, then gave her the thumbs up. She copied me. I led her to the living room's couch, turned on the Firestick, and searched the children's section. The selection hovered over a movie. She shook her head. My phone dinged. Emily reached out her arm to me with an open hand. I put the remote in it and she chose a show two squares down, tucked her feet, and watched entranced.

I hurried back to the dining room and laid on the table. Through the scope was my target typing on her computer. I made my adjustments, my finger to the wall. She pulled her red hair into a bun.

My eyes dashed to Emily, still entranced by her show.

Through the scope I still had my shot. She stood up and walked to the file cabinet, took out a folder, replaced the papers inside, and sat back down.

Emily's laugh caught my attention, but I pulled it back to the scope just in time. Her head was in perfect view. I fired. A pink mist erupted over her desk as she fell forward.

I grinned to myself, but something was off. I turned to Emily. Her eyes, nose, and ballet bun poked above the back of the couch as she stared at me.

I turned my finger to tell her to turn around. She got up and walked to me instead. I sat up and pantomimed taking off the headphones. She handed them to me.

"Are you okay?"

She nodded. "Mhm." She ran her eyes over the gun and looked out the window, then back over the gun. Too late to hide it now.

I wiped her headphones clean and she watched me take apart each piece of the gun and put it away like there'd be a test. I took off the gloves and zipped them in the duffel with everything else.

"Ready?" I asked.

She nodded. We walked in silence to the elevator.

"Do you want to push the button?"

"You killed Uncle Ray, didn't you?" she asked as she pushed the down button. She waited.

"Yes, I did."

"Good." The elevator opened and we got in. "I'm glad he's gone." The elevator closed. She pushed the L button, then took my hand. "Mom's not, but she doesn't know. She keeps thinking he's back, like she hears him or something." She dug her toe into the faux marble.

I gave her hand a squeeze. "He can't hurt you anymore, Emily. I promise."

She looked up at me. "So, you kill people?" Her face was unreadable.

"…Yes."

"Like bad people, right?"

"Yes. The ones who hurt others. Someone needs to stop them. I'm that someone." I swung our enclosed hands.

"So you're the bad guy to bad guys." I looked down at her, but she stared at our reflections in the gold doors holding hands. "You're my hero," she whispered.

The elevator dinged and she skipped by my side through the lobby and out to the street's promenade. "Want to show me your studio?"

"Yes!" She pointed to the left, "It's that way. Come on!" Emily led us back to her mother raging on the phone and pacing in front of Ms. Madison's Dance Extravaganza. "Mommy!" Emily pulled my arm as she ran to her.

Mrs. Rhonestien turned to us and let out a whimper when she saw Emily. "Oh, there she is!" She hung up and dropped to her knees and hugged her daughter close. "Where have you been?!" She glanced up past her bun. "Oh, it's you! What are you doing with Emily?"

"I was down the street when she found me."

"Emily, what have I told you about wandering off?! You scared me to death!"

Emily pulled away, "I didn't go far, Mom."

"You went far enough. We'll talk about this when we get home." She turned to me, "Thank you for bringing her back. Let's go, honey."

"Mommy," Emily pulled her mom to a stop, "can she babysit me? Now that Uncle Ray is gone?"

"Emily!"

"Please, Mom? I'll be good. I swear!"

She raised her brow. "Uh-huh."

"Please? She's nice and fun, and she brought me back. I mean she's cool. And we can do so much fun stuff!" She kept going, and Mrs. Rhonestien looked at me with a sorry expression. We were both trapped.

"I'd love to."

"Yay!"

"Are you sure? I don't want to put a damper on your time. And she can be a lot."

"Don't worry about it, I have a flexible schedule, and I'll keep her safe."

"Thank you. I'll give you a call tomorrow. Come on, honey." Mrs. Rhonestien held out her hand, but Emily ran to me and jumped into a hug.

"Thanks for saving me." She jumped down and took her mom's hand. "See you Wednesday!" We waved to each other till they drove out of sight.

Duck, Duck, Decoy

I screamed and flailed on my bed to get away from the portable air horn my brother aimed at my face. "Tyler!" I threw a pillow at him, which he ducked. "Get out!"

He laughed and tooted it again.

"Give me your key. You're not allowed in here anymore."

"Don't be like that, sis." He sat on the side of the bed and looked around, trying to find what I'd set up this year. "I have to get coffee anyway."

I pulled the blanket over my head.

"Want anything?"

"So they can misspell Shayne on the label again? No, I'm good. Besides, I wouldn't trust it today. You could put laxatives in it like you did three years ago."

"Come on, I never recycle a prank. And I know you can't survive without coffee." If I stayed quiet, he might leave me alone. "Shayne?" I waited for his weight to lift off the bed, to hear retreating footsteps. He tickled me through the blanket.

"Tyler, STOP! Seriously, stop!" I kicked at him and fought with the blanket. I got out and wielded the last pillow on my bed.

"Okay, okay, I'm going!" He ducked and ran. I threw the pillow. It hit his head on his way out. "Ow! Okay! Going!" He laughed. "Be back soon!" He tooted the horn. The front door opened and shut. The lock turned in place and his footsteps ran away.

I groaned. "Note to self, get your housekey away from your brother."

After double checking my coffee, twice, I made a cup, and dressed in something sturdy and comfortable. No telling what he'd pull today. Then I double checked the trap I'd set up in the living room. Cable rope laid hidden in the rug's lining. Bolts and carabiners hung from the walls behind the hanging plants. When the pullies were activated by the app I'd made, they'd pull the couch cover several feet off the ground. I opened the app and checked the game. It was easy enough, for level one. Once the "Congratulations" button was pushed, the pullies would activate.

The key jammed in the doorknob and Tyler came busting into the apartment. He slammed the door shut and locked it.

"Hey, easy on the door." I restarted the app. "I made this new app. I need you to check it out. It's not a prank, I just need your honest opinion. I'm on a deadline."

He peeped through the curtains, careful not to move them too much.

"Tyler?" He continued to watch for something outside. "What are you doing? Where's your coffee?"

"I'm being chased."

I cocked my head to the side and raised my eyebrow. This was his angle? Seriously? "I'm not buying it. Who's chasing you? Bad guys?" I laughed. He didn't.

He pulled back from the window and checked the locks again. "Yes, very bad guys. And if they catch me, they'll kill me."

"Tyler, this is not something to joke about, okay? I know we both agreed to step it up this year, but that's too far."

"This isn't a joke!" He paced from the front door to the couch and back, turned to do it again, saw the window, and paced from the door to the dining room table instead.

"You'd better tell me what's going on."

"I started g…" He took a deep breath and started over. "I started gambling again." He pulled out a chair and sat with his head in his hands.

"How much?"

He looked up with that sorry expression I hadn't seen on him in years. He shook his head and looked down.

"How much?" I asked with force.

"Twenty-five …thousand," he told the carpet.

"Thousa—" I pulled my hand over my mouth. It was my turn to pace.

"I know! I screwed up."

"Screwed up?!"

"Stop it, I know!"

"What did you think you were going to do?"

"Pay it back. In time."

"With what?" He stared at the floor again. "And how much time do you have?"

"A year."

"Good. We can—"

"That was last year. They came looking for me at the coffee shop." I glared at him. "They followed me for a few miles, but I think I lost them." I kicked his butt with my foot.

"You dumbass!" I kicked him again.

"Hey!" He swiped his hand at my foot.

"You idiot!"

"I know, I know! Shayne, I know. Stop it. Enough!"

"Oh, it's not nearly enough!" I swung my foot at him again.

"Stop." He caught my foot and pulled. I hopped after him, swatting at his hand. "Shayne! Knock it off." He stopped and turned to the window. "Stop it. Be quiet."

I looked where he did, and he dropped my foot. We waited for the next sound.

"He's in there," a man said outside the door.

We looked at each other. The doorknob rattled as they picked the lock. I shoved him into the kitchen.

"That's not a way out," he whispered.

"I know. Shush!" I opened the pantry and pushed him to the back. The spice rack hid the door it hung on to another storage area I never used. "Get in there!" I ran to the spare bedroom and opened the sliding door, and ran back to the hiding spot and closed us in. The front door opened, and footsteps came down heavy. I grimaced at the thought of their dirty boots on my white rug.

Tyler's breath caught in his throat. I held his hand.

One of them spoke, "You heard him in here?"

"Yeah," the other answered.

"Check the rooms."

I opened my phone and turned the screen's brightness all the way down.

Tyler hissed, "What are you doing?"

"Seeing what they're doing. Shush." I pulled up my SecureHome app and chose the full camera display. Eight views of the apartment laid out in stacked squares on my screen. The two thugs' matching boots marked my carpet as they stalked around.

"They're checking the bedroom," Tyler whispered.

"Sam, look at this," one shouted. He fluffed his manbun and rubbed the back of his neck as Sam walked in.

"Damn." Sam didn't bother with his blond hair. His lip curled as he took hold of the door frame and leaned out, observing the street. "How far do you think they could be?"

"I don't know. Maybe half a mile if they ran?"

"Wow, John. You're a fucking genius. I mean which direction on the road."

"They could be avoiding roads! I don't know! I was thinking in a circle radius or some shit."

Sam shook his head at John and walked out of the bedroom. John fluffed his manbun again and followed him into the living room. They looked through cabinets, shook out drawers, and looked under tables.

"Nothing. Just a bunch of crap," Sam said.

John sat on the couch. "It is comfortable though. Definitely a woman's home."

Sam cocked his head at him. "Why's that."

"She has decoration stuff. Like the fancy stuff that doesn't do anything but sit there and look pretty."

"Like you."

"Shut up, man." Sam sat next to him on the couch

I selected the living room and it stayed visible as I opened the app I created for my prank.

"What are you doing, Shayne?!"

"Giving us a way out of here."

"They'll leave soon."

John turned on the T.V. and put his boots on the table. "They'll be back eventually. Once they think we're gone."

I raised my brow at Tyler. He raised his arms in a shrug.

"Watch this." I played the first level, reaching the end in seconds. The congratulations button rose up in a flurry of rainbow-colored confetti. I pressed it. The pullies activated. John's feet swung over his head as the couch cushion cover lifted them both into the air. They were trapped, suspended several feet off the ground like a sack of bad guy potatoes.

"You said that wasn't a prank," Tyler pointed at the game.

"Not now." I lead us out and we headed for the front door. "Thanks for dropping in, boys. Feel free to hang around."

Shouts through clenched jaws came from the suspended sack, and it started to sway as they kicked and clawed to get out. I grabbed the car keys and locked the door behind us.

"We have to go to the police station." I drove just enough over the speed limit to get some distance.

"No, we can't do that. These guys would easily kill me in prison. No police."

"Goddamnit, Tyler! They broke into my apartment!"

"I know. I'm sorry!"

"No, that's not gonna cut it. They destroyed my rug, and whatever else of mine going through my stuff. What were they looking for?"

"Remember when I helped Mom with Grandpa's garage sale three years ago? Well I kept a couple things."

"Oh, this just keeps getting better and better."

"It wasn't like Mom didn't know." He shifted in his seat. "It was just some stuff she didn't think would sell. One of them was a wooden duck decoy. We didn't know how valuable they could get. Most of them are worth maybe a hundred to a few hundred, but the

91

ones in good condition by certain companies are worth a lot. And remember Grandma kept everything so clean? It's in great condition."

"How much is it worth?"

"About forty thousand."

"Enough to settle your debt, with interest. Where is it?"

"Mom's house."

"Seriously?!"

"I didn't want to lose it."

I sighed. "Okay. Mom's it is."

Tyler called her on our way. She was thrilled we were coming over. I asked if we could park in the garage, which weirded her out, but she agreed. I didn't want to risk my car leading anyone to her.

"Come on in and sit down. I'm glad you both stopped by, but I'm guessing there's a reason."

"Yeah, there is. Do you know where you put that duck decoy I kept from Grandpa?"

"Oh, that old thing. You left it here, so I thought you didn't want it anymore. I gave it to Cathy down the street."

Tyler pushed out a sigh as his head fell back to the couch.

"She came over for my dinner party last week. Went off without a hitch! Everyone loved that durian quiche recipe you two aren't fond of. Honestly, the both of you are the pickiest eaters I know. It's supposed to be good for you. But I think if you just gave it another try…"

A faded, orange, beat up car passed the house. Sam drove as John looked around.

"We'll try it next time, but we should really get going." I nudged Tyler.

"What?"

Idiot.

"Oh, don't run off. I just put some in the microwave. I tweaked the recipe a bit. I added cheese. The kind you guys like."

I stood up and knocked his foot with mine. He stood too. "Sorry, Mom, we really can't stay, we were just stopping by. It smells good though. Can we take them to go?"

She smiled. "Sure! Let me get a tub to put them in." She got up and went to the kitchen.

"They do not smell good," he said under his breath.

"Duh. But it's the only thing that'll get us out the door."

She came back with a Tupperware container. "Here. Let me know what you think of them."

"We will. And we'll be there for family dinner next week."

Tyler kissed her cheek. "Thanks, Mom."

"Ugh, Tyler don't open that in the car!"

"I was just curious." I rolled down the window. "How much further to Cathy's?"

"See that house with the green roof? That's the one. Looks like she's having a party."

"And she didn't invite Mom…" We exchanged a look and he held up the container with a grin. I nodded.

A couple parked their car and walked into the house without ringing the bell. We followed. The house was packed with people in their summer's best, holding glasses of various wines. Every surface displayed pretty food on platters. Cathy's husband tended the barbeque surrounded by "the boys". Every now and then there was tasteful laughter and the clinking of glasses. We snuck into the kitchen and found a decorative glass platter waiting on the counter. We opened the container and laid out the durian quiches in a spiral, then took it to the main table and swapped it with her center dish of tea sandwiches, which we put out of the way in the living room. We high fived and then split up to look for the duck. I took upstairs, he took downstairs.

After an hour of searching I get a TikTok from Tyler dancing with the duck decoy on his shoulder in the downstairs bathroom. He texted that he'd meet me by the stairs. I headed down and stopped dead on the staircase. I knew that manbun. John and Sam walked into the kitchen as Tyler rounded the corner from the hallway. I jumped the last few steps.

"Let's go."

"Don't you want to see someone try to eat those?" He pointed at the food we set.

"We don't have time. They're here."

They walked out of the kitchen and locked eyes with us. Sam moved forward and John followed. Without breaking eye contact, John swiped a quiche and stuck the whole thing in his mouth. He stopped walking. His face scrunched up in a gag, and he threw up. Sam turned around. We shoved our way past the gathering crowd to the front door.

"What the hell's going on here?!" Cathy shouted.

We slipped out and high fived on our way to the car.

"So now what?" I asked. "Do we auction this thing online or …?"

He set up his phone with GPS. "I have a guy."

"Of course you do."

"You know what, can you stop with the judging me and stuff? I know how badly I messed up here. Okay? You don't have to rub it in my face."

"I just want to know why you did it. I mean, was all this worth it? Putting me in danger? Mom? You?! Did you think it'd be worth it when you somehow racked up a debt of twenty thousand dollars?"

He rocked the duck between his hands on his lap. "Twenty-five thousand."

My fingers splayed from the wheel. "Oh my god."

He sighed and leaned back into the seat. "I didn't think it'd get this out of control. I had the money to pay it back, but then my car broke down, rent was due. Things just caught up to me."

I shook my head. "You hid it well this time. I didn't know you started gambling again till those guys showed up at my apartment. How long has this been going on for? I thought you were doing okay?"

"I was. For a while. It was just that one time. I started winning, and I had it under control."

"And then you didn't."

"And then I didn't."

The GPS chimed in, "You have arrived."

"Well this is the creepiest parking garage I've ever seen."

"It's reputable."

"Give me the duck." He handed it over and we got out of the car.

"The auction house is through here." Tyler pointed to the set of glass doors.

"Hold it right there!" Car brakes screeched behind us.

We froze.

The doors opened and closed. "Turn around. Slowly." We turned to see Sam and John pointing guns at us. "Tyler," Sam continued, "do you have the money?"

"Yeah." He took the duck from me and held it up for them.

He squinted at it.

"I don't believe them," said John. "I'm done with this shit."
He aimed his gun at Tyler.

"Wait!" I shouted. "The money's in the duck."

"What do you mean in the duck?!"

"Yeah, I'm not buying it either."

"There's a hatch on the bottom. We stuffed the money in there. We were just taking it in to be counted."

Tyler shot a sideways glance at me.

Sam motioned with his gun. "Open it."

"Go on," I nodded, "open it."

He shook his head and turned it over, lifting the latch to the hidden compartment. He pulled out the piece of paper that was inside. "It's a note."

"Read it," Sam said. "Out loud."

He unfolded it and read. "Tyler, I paid your debt, you dumbass. Don't do this shit again or next time it could be real. I love you. Happy April Fools. Shayne." He looked at me.

Sam and John shot him, with their water guns. He jumped and screamed. My laugh echoed in the garage. They stopped when I got my breath.

"Thanks, guys! This was the great. Really. I'll see you at work."

"No problem." Sam smiled. He and John walked back to their car.

"Where'd you get that thing, anyway?" I waived at their orange monstrosity.

"Craigslist."

"Can you return it?" We laughed.

"Hold on! So, this whole time, you knew?! And you guys are—"

"Her friends from work," John piped in. "Nice to meet you." They got in their car and drove off, waving to us.

"What the hell, Shayne! How could you do this to me?"

"Do this to you?! You did this to yourself! And the one thing you never considered is what it would do to anyone else. Two guys actually did come to my apartment looking for you to settle your debt, about three weeks ago. They weren't like today, they stayed in the doorway, but it was terrifying. And a shock to me. I thought you were good. Imagine my surprise at two random men showing up at my apartment. I'm not even sure how they found me!"

He looked at his feet.

"I paid them. You're free and clear."

His gripped the duck and note in his hands. "Thank you."

I grinned. "You're also not allowed back. If you do, we agreed they'd take you directly to my house, every time. They've spread the word."

He laughed. "Thanks."

"Now let's get this duck sold so we can go home."

"You still want to do that?"

"I have a gap in my bank account that needs to be fixed. And we could get some lunch after." We walked to the set of glass doors.

"You're not going to put laxatives in it, right?"

I shrugged. "There's still time."

About the Author

Jane P. Eris, short story writer and novelist of speculative a psychological fiction. Eris has been featured in publications since 2013. She began writing her first novel, in math class, in her senior year of high school. From there, her writing has taken her on a decade long adventure that's just beginning. The short stories in this collection have been plucked from that adventure since its origin of her first publication with *Currents Vol. 47*, "The Present".